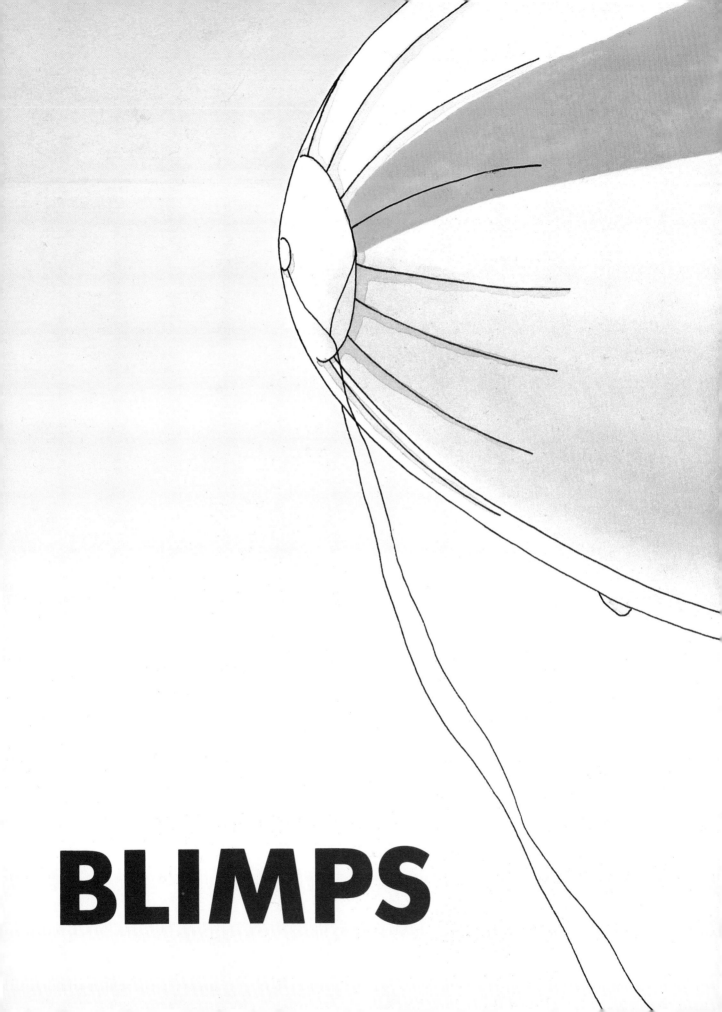

BLIMPS

E. P. DUTTON · NEW YORK

BLIMPS
ROXIE MUNRO

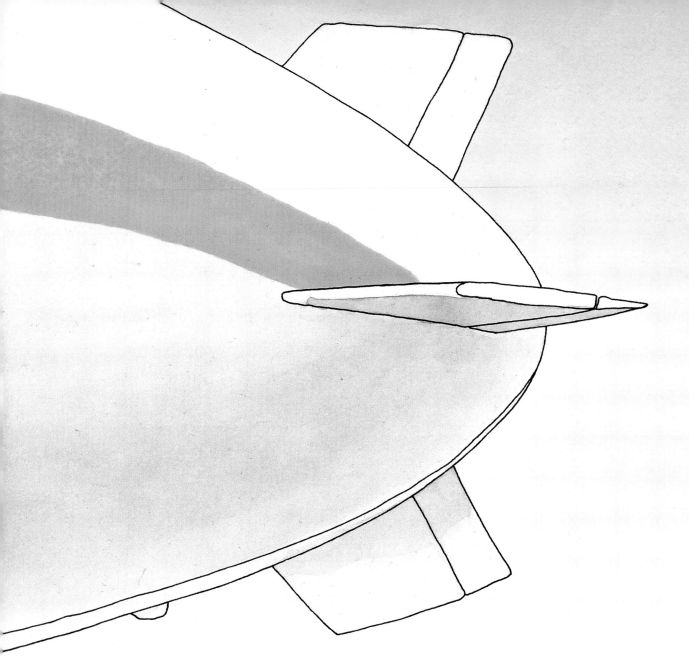

Copyright © 1989 by Roxie Munro

All rights reserved.

Published in the United States by E. P. Dutton,
2 Park Avenue, New York, N.Y. 10016,
a division of NAL Penguin Inc.

Published simultaneously in Canada by
Fitzhenry & Whiteside Limited, Toronto

Designer: Alice Lee Groton

Printed in the U.S.A.   W   First Edition
10 9 8 7 6 5 4 3 2 1

Library of Congress Cataloging-in-Publication Data

Munro, Roxie.
Blimps.

Summary: Discusses the construction, design,
operation, and uses of blimps and how it feels
to ride in one.
1. Airships—Juvenile literature. [1. Airships]
I. Title.
TL656.2.M86 1988 629.133′24 88-18138
ISBN 0-525-44441-6

Thanks to Donna Brooks, my editor; Bo Zaunders, my husband; Jonothan Logan for his scientific advice and
many suggestions; Carol S. O'Loughlin of Fuji Photo Film U.S.A., Inc.; Fuji Photo Film U.S.A., Inc., for the use
of *Airship Fuji*; Alix Cochrane, Mary Lee Dickson, Gardner Craft, and John Hankinson of Airship Industries
(U.S.A.); George A. Spyrou of Airship Industries (U.K.); all the other helpful people at Airship Industries on
both sides of the Atlantic; and Don Ploskunak and Michael Wittman of the Goodyear Tire and Rubber Company.

No one knows for
sure just where the word *blimp* comes
from. It may have originated with a Lieutenant A. D.
Cunningham, who commanded a British airship station during
World War I. The story goes that while inspecting an airship used
to scout German submarines, he playfully reached out and flicked
his thumb against the gasbag. A funny noise echoed off the
fabric. ''Blimp,'' he said, imitating the sound and amusing
the station crew. And blimp it has
been ever since.

A blimp begins as a big polyester bag, like a giant limp balloon. When it is inflated with the gas helium, it will rise.

Air, a mixture of gases, weighs very little. But helium weighs even less—about one-seventh as much. This difference allows helium-filled blimps to float on the sea of air around us, much as ships float on the earth's oceans, and even to carry loads of 500 kilograms (a half ton) or more.

Blimps do not float willy-nilly like balloons, wherever wind and air currents take them. They are pushed through the air by their engine-driven propellers, and steered by rudders on their tail fins. Aircraft that are self-propelled, steerable, and borne aloft by a gas that is lighter than air are called airships, or dirigible balloons. In the past, many airships had stiff, rigid frameworks. A blimp is a nonrigid airship. Its beautiful, voluminous shape is maintained only by the pressure of the helium within.

Blimps are blown up and assembled in the largest hangars in the world. One hangar is more than three times the length of a football field—so big that workers sometimes use a bicycle to get around. The gasbag, also called the envelope or balloon, arrives at the hangar all folded up in a big box. Workers carefully remove and unfold it to get it ready for inflation. The gasbag is actually made of thirty or so strips of material, or gores, each a little more than a half meter (about 20 inches) wide and as long as the blimp—anywhere from 52 to 63 meters (about 165 to 205 feet), depending on the blimp's design. To keep the envelope as light and smooth as possible, the gores do not overlap. They abut and are glued together. The gastight fabric usually has a coating to protect it from the sun's rays.

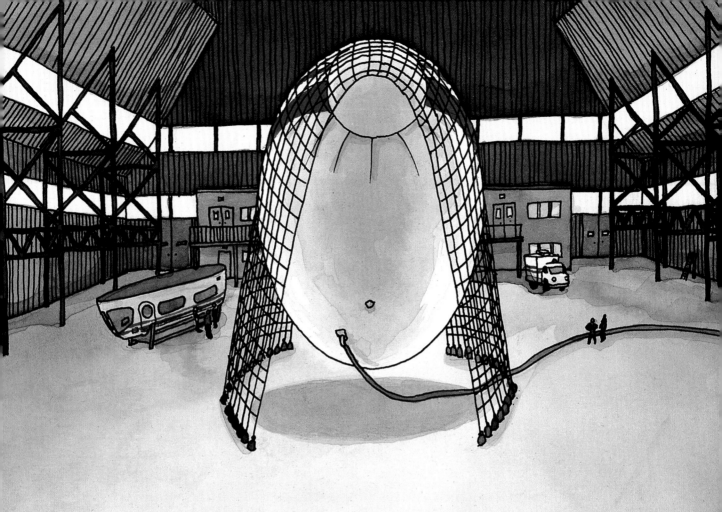

Helium is trucked to the hangar in large tanks. It is a safe, stable gas—unlike hydrogen, a gas formerly used in airships. Hydrogen bursts into flames at the slightest spark, but helium never burns. Over the next eight hours it passes through a hose into the gasbag, and the gasbag gradually swells.

As it swells, the gasbag pushes the air around it out of the way. The air pushed aside is pulled downward by the force of gravity, which is always pulling everything on earth to the ground. The bag of helium is pulled downward also, but not as strongly, for helium weighs less than air. By the time the gasbag is completely filled with helium, it has pushed aside, or displaced, a volume of air as big as, but weighing more than, itself. As this volume of air is drawn downward by gravity, it pushes the gasbag up, out of the way. And so the gasbag floats. In the hangar, a safety net keeps it from bumping the ceiling.

A blimp usually takes off from a field at a small airport. Until takeoff, it is moored by its reinforced nose to the mast of a special truck carrying other equipment for the mooring. The nose cone and its radiating ribs are laced onto the gasbag after it is inflated.

Pilots and passengers travel in the gondola, a boat-shaped cabin underneath the balloon, also attached after inflation. The balloon itself contains nothing but gas—about 5,000 to 7,000 cubic meters of it (175,000 to 245,000 cubic feet).

Why is the balloon so big? The power of a blimp to rise and lift things is equal to the weight of the air it displaces. A helium-filled party balloon only displaces about 6 grams (⅕ ounce) of air—it cannot lift much more than the string attached to it. But a blimp is meant to lift thousands of kilograms. So it must displace air weighing at least that much. How does it do this? By being *big*. Blimps are big because air is light.

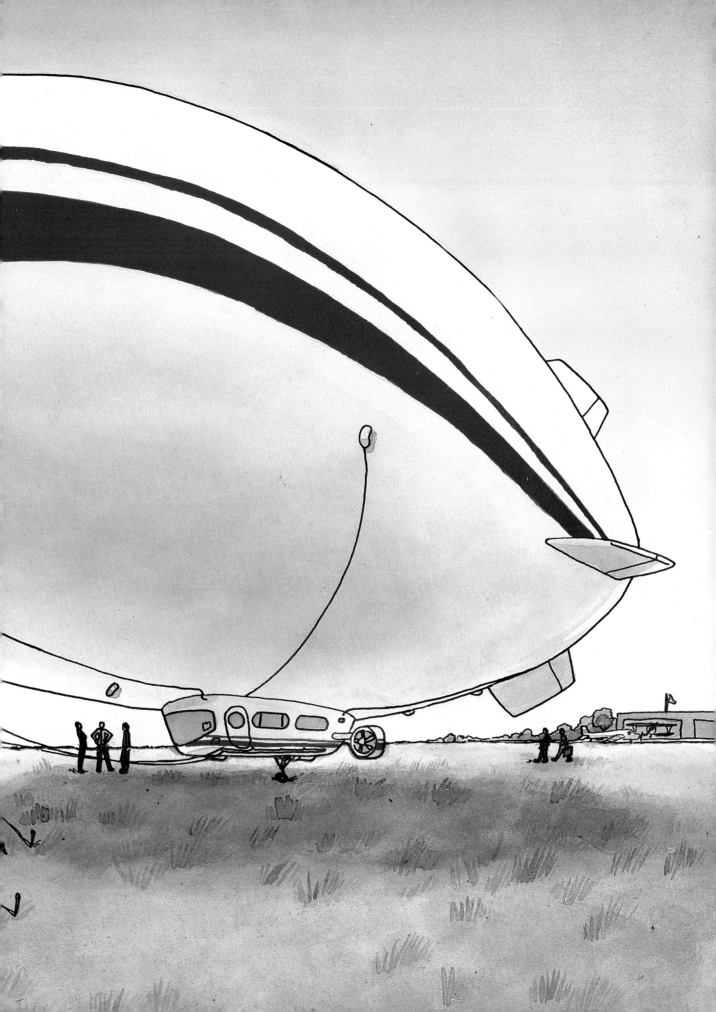

A moored blimp responds freely to the breeze, rotating around its mast like a huge wind sock. Rocking and turning, it can seem almost alive. There is something charming, even faintly clownish, about this tremendous bobbing balloon. And there is something innocent and otherworldly, too, as if it were only momentarily linked to the earth and eager to be off again. Climb on under its belly, and it will loft you away to its airy habitat.

The pilot and copilot get on first and start the engines. Then passengers mount the ladder. Some of the ground crew steady the blimp, holding the gondola's railings. Others take hold of the bowlines, two heavy ropes that trail from the nose of the blimp at all times.

A gondola seats between seven and twenty people, depending on the design of the blimp. It is constructed from manmade materials that are sturdy but light, and attached to the balloon by suspension cables and strong glue. The tail fins are made of material similar to the gondola and are laced to the envelope.

Blimps are constructed to be as lightweight as possible. Except for valve fittings and the cockpit instruments, the only metal on the blimp is the steel on two engines, each about the size of a car engine, at the rear of the gondola.

How fast the blimp will rise or descend depends on the exact balance between the amount of helium in the balloon and the load it carries. So the pilot and ground crew pay careful attention to the weight of everyone and everything that comes on board. Inside the gondola, small canvas bags filled with lead shot (tiny beads of lead) help keep the blimp from rising. Each of these ballast bags weighs 10 kilograms (about 22 pounds). As passengers get on, ballast bags equaling their weight are removed. Sometimes passengers actually step on a scale before boarding, but in any case the ground crew is usually adept at judging weight just by looking.

When it's time for takeoff, one of the ground crew unlocks the blimp from its mast, and the people holding the bowlines pull the blimp, nose into the wind.

At a hand signal from the pilot, the bowlines are let go,
the blimp quickly rises, and the earth drops away.

On some blimps it's possible to see into the balloon through a domed window in the gondola ceiling. In this picture, the envelope has been cut away so you can see inside.

What if you could actually get inside? You would not be able to see, smell, or taste the helium gas. It has no color, no odor, no flavor. But if you took a breath, you could tell it was there. A lungful would not poison or hurt you. It would make your voice sound high, because sound travels faster in a light gas like helium than it does in air.

But you could not breathe helium for very long before you would faint. Your body would soon be starved of oxygen, one of the gases in air that all animals need in order to live. There is air in a large polyester or rubber pouch at each end of the balloon. These two airbags, or ballonets, automatically adjust the pressure inside the balloon. As the blimp rises, the atmosphere gets thinner and no longer presses against the balloon as strongly as the helium presses out. To prevent the expanding helium from straining the envelope, air is emptied from the ballonets into the atmosphere. As the blimp descends, electric fans force air back into the ballonets. They can also be controlled from the cockpit. By having more air in one ballonet than the other, the pilot can point the nose up or down, or "trim" the airship.

The cables you see help support the gondola. They extend from extra fabric glued to the top of the balloon through gastight fittings at the bottom.

Riding in a blimp is very different from riding in a plane. A blimp flies low and slowly. Passengers feel suspended in air. They can see houses, toll booths, schools, and parking lots, but they cannot see the blimp that is carrying them. Compared to the sleek, sealed space of a jetliner cabin and the powerful roar of jet engines, being in the small gondola with its broad windows, simple fixtures, and purring propellers can be almost scary at first.

In ideal weather, a blimp flies smoothly through the air. But in windy patches or updrafts, it can pitch and roll like a sailboat dipping through the waves.

In bad weather, such as rain or snow or wind over 25 knots (28 miles per hour), a blimp remains moored to its mast. It can fly if rain or wind come up while it is airborne, but a pilot would not choose to take off in such weather.

A blimp usually flies 300 to 1,000 meters (1,000 to 3,000 feet) above the ground, with a ceiling—the highest a blimp can go—of about 3 kilometers (2 miles). The average speed is 25 to 35 knots (28 to 40 miles per hour), although in a blimp race down the Hudson River to the Statue of Liberty, the winning blimp traveled at 50 knots (56 miles per hour).

On trips of several hours, the ground crew stays behind at the landing field. But on trips from one city to another, extra pilots and the ground crew follow the blimp. They travel in an equipment-packed caravan of pickups, vans, a jeep, a bus, or even an eighteen-wheeler. And, of course, the all-important mast truck, so the blimp can be moored wherever it lands. The crew tries to keep the blimp in sight and always maintains radio contact.

Come fall and winter, blimps and their crews migrate to warmer climates, not unlike other creatures of the air. In Europe they go to one of the Mediterranean countries. In the United States, they head for California, Texas, or Florida, and in the spring travel east and north again. Flying eight hours a day, tying down at night, a blimp can cross the country in a few weeks. One blimp took as long as thirty-three days, because bad weather prevented flying on all but thirteen of them.

Each day the pilot must decide if it is safe to fly. If it is, the blimp glides serenely over factories and fields, rivers and roads, even beside skyscrapers.

Slow and steady, blimps make stable platforms for cameras. If you have watched sports on television, you have probably seen aerial views photographed from a blimp. When the pilot slows the engines to hover over a stadium or tennis court or raceway, a cameraman, often shooting from an open gondola window, experiences almost no vibration.

Companies rent blimps as giant floating billboards, displaying their names in huge letters that can be read a mile away. People like to look at blimps, and they often feel an odd affection for them, so a blimp is probably a good place to advertise. Most signs are detachable banners, since repainting the envelope over and over would add weight. The banners are tied to rings glued to the sides of the balloon. Some blimps have computer-controlled grids with thousands of tiny light bulbs that display animated images as well as words to light up the night sky. And sometimes the two companies that have made most of the world's blimps—the Goodyear Tire and Rubber Company, and Airship Industries—display their own names.

Sightseeing tours by blimp are beginning to be offered over some of the world's major cities. San Francisco, London, Munich, and Sydney have already had touring blimps in their skies.

A blimp can operate for nearly a week on the fuel a jet plane uses to taxi down the runway and take off. A jet needs powerful engines to propel it forward at high speeds and keep it in the air. But a blimp is buoyed upward effortlessly by the air itself. It needs engines mainly to push it forward.

Traveling close to the earth, you can see a lot from a blimp. Blimps have been used to patrol coastlines, to study the sea, and to keep track of air, noise, and oil pollution. Blimps can service pipelines, power cables, and offshore oil rigs. During World Wars I and II, blimps flew thousands of antisubmarine escort missions and performed search-and-rescue work. Several crossed the Atlantic Ocean, although blimps today are too small to carry the amount of fuel required for that journey. With its scant metal, a blimp is hard for radar to detect. And a blimp is more durable than it looks. Even if the envelope is punctured, the helium inside escapes very slowly. A blimp can fly for hours with a hole the size of a saucer in it.

When the day's journey is done and it's time to descend, the pilot adjusts flaps on the tail fins to point the nose downward, and may also add air to the forward ballonet.

On the ground, the crew lines up to form a human V, with the wind to the back of the man at the point, the ground crew chief. No matter where and when a blimp lands—and blimps are assembled and flown on four continents—the ground crew always lines up like this. It makes an easy target for the pilot, and it ensures that the wind is in front of the blimp, helping to slow it down—not at the sides or behind, where it might make landing fast and unpredictable.

Some blimps carry water as emergency ballast in a tank at the back of the gondola. If the pilot sees that the blimp is coming in too fast and is going to land with too much impact, he can quickly make it lighter by opening "dump valves" connected to the tank, spilling out the water. Occasionally the ground crew gets a surprise shower.

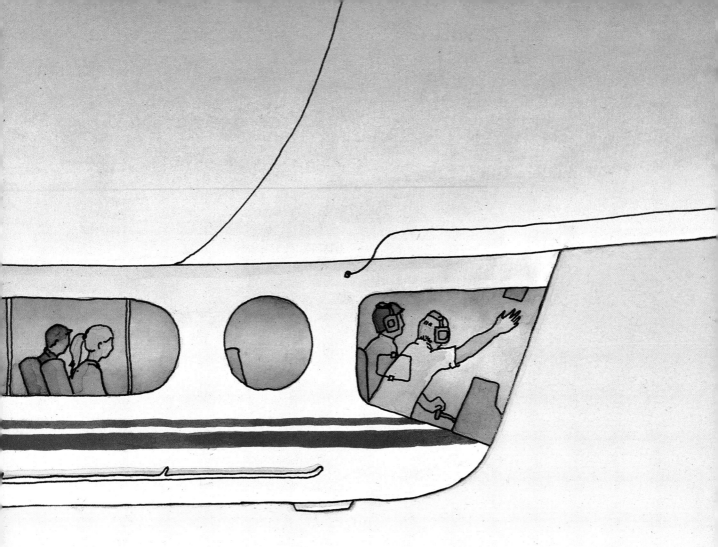

Flying in a blimp is a lot like flying in your dreams.

Blimp pilots are usually airplane or helicopter pilots with extra training. But they say that flying a blimp is more like skippering a sailboat or a submarine—a sailboat, because of the blimp's sensitivity to wind; a submarine, because a blimp uses air to trim in the same way a submarine uses water as ballast to surface or dive.

To land, the pilot aims for the point of the V. To help cushion the landing, ground crew members grab the gondola railings. Others take hold of the bowlines and maneuver the blimp to its mooring mast. The blimp is locked on, and ballast bags are brought back on board.

One member of the ground crew stays with the blimp, spending the night on the mast truck. That person monitors the helium pressure inside the balloon as the temperature and weather change, and makes sure everything is all right.

Once inflated, a blimp is rarely deflated. Moored outside in all but heavy snow or a hurricane, it waits for the call to rise.